# WHAT PEOPLE ARE SAYING:

*Chance* is a collection of stories dwelling in the dark side of the human psyche. It is unsettling, fascinating, and impossible to put down.

Nan Wisherd, Author of *Pathways, The Earliest History of Northern Wisconsin's Brule Region, Echoes From the Past, and Brule River Country,* www.cablepublishing.com.

Joyce's noir collection is not for the Pollyannaish. Take off those rosy blinders and wade into the depths of life's darkest. See through the eyes of sick, twisted weirdoes and everyday folks who churn through life motivated by desires and rages ... you may just find a little bit of yourself looking back at you from the pages. What you see in her book's mirror may shock you. Do you dare wander into these blackened edges of your own awareness?

Mike Angley, Special Agent (USAF, ret), Colonel (USAF, ret), Award-winning Author of the *Child Finder Trilogy,* www.mikeangley.com

Joyce Faulkner takes the reader on a journey through a slice of society unknown to most. A chilling glimpse into disturbed minds. An alternate title might be *Tales from the Macabre Zone*.

I found the stories to be haunting—hard to forget—unsettling. Steven King has competition.

Lee Boyland, author of *The Rings of Allah, Behold, an Ashen Horse, America Reborn,* and *Pirates and Cartels*.

Award-winning author Joyce Faulkner proves once again that she is a master storyteller. In this stunning new collection of short stories, "Chance: And Other Horrors," Ms. Faulkner lures you in from the get go. Normally a scaredy-cat when it comes to reading horror stories, I was apprehensive about taking a chance on "Chance." Then I read the opening line, and I was sucked right in. The author knows how to tempt the reader and gain empathy. Not an easy task in any genre.

Kathleen M. Rodgers, author of numerous newspaper and magazine articles and the award-winning novel, *The Final Salute: Together We Live On*.

# CHANCE

## and other horrors

# Joyce
# Faulkner

### Including
### "Unforgivable"

ISBN: Paperback:     978-0-9834930-0-6

E-book:     978-0-9827923-8-4

LCCN:          2011924724

Cover Design: Joyce Faulkner

The Page Turns

Printed in the United States

*While I know that there can be no up without a down and no light without darkness, these are the fears that visit my nightmares and questions that haunt my dreams. They make me appreciate sanity...*

*Joyce Faulkner*

# CONTENTS

# CHANCE

I saw her again last night at long last—a graceful phantom striding across my path, her long white hair glowing like a beacon in the low beams of my Volvo. My erection saluted her resilient beauty. I didn't understand myself—she had to be 75 by now.

My bad leg slipped off the clutch. The car lurched and died. Hannah glanced over her shoulder and her chilly blue eyes met mine. No recognition. She continued across the street with the pace of a much younger woman. I gaped at her with the lust of a much younger man. She disappeared into a house two doors down from the intersection.

I drove to the bare apartment I called home and limped to the fridge to collect my first Bass Ale of the evening. Sitting on a sliver of deck outside my sliding glass doors, I dreamed of Hannah—my cock rising and falling in cadence with my memories.

My father, Arlen Martindale, found Hannah when I was eighteen. They both said they knew it was love when Hannah burst into the office of my Dad's Mobile Home business and inquired about the *Sunrise Special*. They were married three weeks later on a Thursday afternoon at the local bowling alley. She never did buy a trailer.

Whatever else you can say about Hannah, she made my father happy. I could see it in the way he touched the flesh of her upper arm. Once, I came home from the bookstore at lunchtime and caught them entwined on the couch. They sat up—straightening their clothes like guilty teenagers.  Dad actually blushed. I pretended not to notice and hobbled into the kitchen for a sandwich.

I never knew what broke them up. One day, eighteen months later, Hannah slipped out before breakfast leaving Dad a note telling him where to send her clothes. We sat at the kitchen table eating oatmeal. When he finished, he stared out the window.

"I'm sorry, Dad." I wished it was okay to hug him.

He shrugged and sipped his coffee. "Back to work." He set the mug down solidly on the counter like a punctuation point.

When Hannah was with Dad that first time, I never really noticed her. She was my step-mom—no way could she replace my rosy-faced mother who died when I was ten. Mostly I ignored her.

Then one day she came into the bookstore. It was November 14, 1962—a rainy Wednesday morning. She shook water out of the plastic babushka women wore to protect their bouffant hairdos in those days. Her hair was dark then—twisting and swirling around the crown of her head. Stiff springy bangs decorated her forehead just above her jeweled glasses.

"Hi, Chance. Why don't we do lunch?"

"Me?" My own glasses slid down my nose. I pushed them up with a band-aid covered finger.

"You think you could make time for me?" I noticed her pointy breasts under her pink sweater along about then. She was only a little taller than me, but in her spike-heeled shoes I stared at her lips and chin mostly. My heart pounded.

I held a broken-spined umbrella over us and struggled to keep up with her long-legged stride. We found a corner booth at Maxine's Café two blocks from the bookstore. I ordered lemonade with my sandwich—she drank hot tea.

"Chance, I need you to bring me some papers from Arlen's desk. I feel funny about calling him given the situation." She leaned forward and her nipples grazed the table.

"What do you need?" My eyes were fixed on her bosom.

"There's an envelope marked "Insurance" in the middle drawer. I put all my tax records in it. We're coming up on the end of the year, so I'm going to need them."

"Okay."

"Are you paying attention, Chance? Yes, I see that you are." She pulled her slant-eyed, black-framed glasses off and laughed, rocking her shoulders to make her breasts jiggle.

"Oh, Hannah." I could barely force the words out. "I'm sorry."

"How old are you?"

"Twenty. Almost twenty." I stared at my hands, the tips of my ears burning.

"You look so much younger—not a trace of a beard." She reached across the table and touched my cheek. I flinched. "Have you ever had a woman, Chance?"

I shook my head.

"Why not?"

"I don't know. My leg -- ." I shrugged.

"This is one sport where you don't need your leg, buddy." I peeked up at her through my lashes. She puckered her mouth and made a kissing noise. "Okay, let's go, big boy." Leaving five dollars on the table to pay for lunch, she stood and held out her hand to me. When I didn't take it, she slipped her fingers through mine and pulled me to my feet. I was breathing heavily.

The windshield wipers bumped back and forth on her green fifty-six Chevy. We turned down an overgrown, muddy path just outside of town and parked under a pine tree.

Even now, I remember she smelled like warm vanilla and her body quivered when I touched it. I couldn't get over that. It was pretty heady stuff—a grown woman giving herself to me. Thirty years later, I can't breathe when I think about it.

When it was over, she pinched my cheek and laughed. "Now he's a great big man, isn't he?"

I looked away. She used the rearview mirror to retouch her makeup and pat stray sprigs of hair back into the beehive.

"We better get you back home." She put the car in reverse and backed around the tree. Staring out the window as we headed for town, I sniffed my hand from time to time. She pulled up in front of the bookstore.

"Thanks, Hannah." I didn't know what else to say.

A week later, she went back to Dad. I didn't even realize it the first night, but there she was at breakfast, eating oatmeal with us. I glanced from one to the other. Neither of them offered an explanation. I'd never got around to taking her that envelope.

Dad was happy again. He went to work late and came home early. Hannah met him at the door and threw her arms around his neck. He squeezed her buttocks with thick-fingered hands as if he were staking a claim. One night, he came into the living room where I sat reading and winked like he knew a secret I didn't. Hannah followed him into the room. She looked at me, her mouth twitching at the corners.

Most nights I lay in bed trying to block out the image of him taking her. I pulled a pillow over my head to drown out the muffled moans and slow squeaking sounds coming from his room. Standing naked in front of my mirrored closet door, I examined my deficiencies. A thin, white manikin with one leg longer than the other, I leaned to the right like some Italian tower. I was too young and crippled to compete.

Every morning, Dad and I left the house while Hannah stayed home to do whatever it was she did. She quit her job as an Insurance Agent the same day she came back. That must have pleased

Dad. He whistled as he drove me to work.

I priced and stacked books pretending she wanted me. I ran the register dreaming she came back for me, not him. It was hopeless. I grew to hate my own father.

I fancied I was no longer welcome at the dinner table. He wanted to be alone with his prize. The three of us sat quietly in the candlelight. Hannah focused on Dad—filling his plate with the best morsels—asking after his health—gazing at him with the eyes of a newlywed. Once in a while, she'd glance my way. I hated her too.

And then, Dad had to go to market to pick out which units 'Martindale Mobile Homes' would offer in the spring of 1963. He packed his bags, kissed Hannah one last lingering time and was off for the big city.

Hannah drove me to work. Before I got out of the Chevy, she ran her long-nailed fingers inside my thigh and peered at me over her glasses. That evening, I came home to Hannah and took Dad's place in her bed. The whole night was mine. I acted out every fantasy Hannah had ignited that November afternoon in the woods.

"Oh Chance!" She moaned under my lips. "I've wanted you so much. I came back for you. It was always you. I endured him to get back to you."

Filled with the passion of youth, I believed her. I wanted to believe.

"Will you marry me?" I sat on the side of my father's bed, rubbing my bad leg, her scent clogging my mind.

"I'm already married, Chance." She sighed. "If only I'd met you first."

"You can leave him. You did once."

"How do you think he would feel if I left him for you? It would hurt him. If I could only do it without him knowing." Hannah knelt behind me on the bed, her breasts pressing against my back. Her flesh stirred me again. I was twenty. Her dramatic tone sounded right to me then.

I left her curled up naked under the quilt my grandmother made for my mother's hope chest. Her glasses lay on the nightstand along with her Timex and a two-month old 'Glamour' magazine. For all our athletic lovemaking, her upswept hairdo remained in place, her make-up untouched. Her snore was a soft 'brrrrrr' as I closed the door behind me.

I hopped downstairs and took three bottles of Dad's Budweiser out of the old Kelvinator. The first one made a satisfying 'pop' and then 'sssss' when I opened it. I went out onto the back porch and sat in a painted lawn chair trying to remember I loved my Dad. He coached Little League all those years when I was a kid. Of course, I was never able to play. I was just the batboy.

I opened the second beer and sniffed my fingers. The thought of him savoring that sweetness enraged me. He was an experienced player. I doubted I could bat against him directly. I needed subterfuge and a fury fueled by testosterone and madness. It turns out I had plenty of both.

The next night I beat Arlen Martindale to death with a baseball bat when he stepped through the door. I remember the look on his face when I first swung. When he was dead, I limped over to the couch and sat down panting. Blood spatters covered the walls—and me. I shuddered. Hannah called the police.

I went willingly to prison. I was numb—my passion for Hannah died with my father—splashed on the floor in our hallway. She never came to see me anyway. She owned the house my father built when I was a baby. She put her things in my Mother's hope chest. She even inherited 'Martindale Mobile Homes.'

I served two years before I realized Hannah killed Dad for insurance and I was her weapon. In the thirteenth year of my sentence, I understood there are all kinds of passion.

It took ten years to find her after I got out of prison. After all, she could live anywhere she pleased. She took out two million dollars in whole life before she left him the first time. When Arlen Martindale died, it was double indemnity —no questions asked. I was small and boyish, crippled—a loner. No one guessed she used me. Not even me. They thought I went crazy on my own.

I sat on the deck, my legs dangling through the railing, sucking down beer after beer. At midnight, I threw my bat into the back of the Volvo and drove to her house. I parked on a side street. Holding the bat inside my coat, I crept up to her door and rang the bell.

The porch light came on. "Who is it?" Her voice had deepened with age and cigarettes.

"Chance Martindale." I was no longer skinny. My black hair had thinned on top. I wore contacts and an orthopedic shoe. I was erect and straight. I looked normal.

She opened the door smiling. Her nipples glowed through the sheer fabric of her nightgown. She was confident of her allure—even now. Maturity was subtle in her face. Soft lines radiated from her eyes and her lips. A slight stoop in her shoulders was the only concession her body made to age. Her snowy white hair shimmered in the moonlight when I first swung the bat.

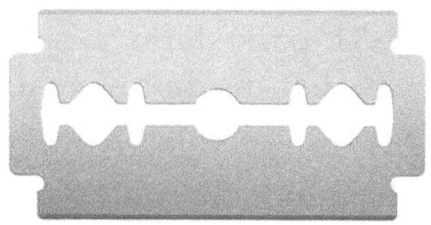

# MORNING SMILED

A light flickered behind the bathroom shade. Otis crouched in the bushes outside the open window. The young woman whimpered. He rose up and peered through the screen.

A purple candle dripped smoky wax onto the linoleum. Morning sat naked at the foot of the commode. She stared at her left forearm where dark blood oozed from a series of shallow slices. She sighed and leaned back against the chipped tub, her legs stretched out in front of her. Still holding the razor blade between her thumb and forefinger, her right arm dropped to the floor beside her thigh.

Otis backed away. He crept through the chest-high Rhododendrons guarding her backyard and staggered to his car in the alley. Sweat cooled on his neck and raised gooseflesh on his arms. He pounded the steering wheel with his fist.

Something moved in Morning's backyard. Otis squinted. A dark figure slipped through the Rhododendrons Otis had just left.

⌂⌂⌂

Otis moved the cash register to the far end of the counter so he could see her flip burgers in the coffee shop across the street. He sat on a tall stool and sold greeting cards to blue-haired ladies with big pocket books while he stared out the front window.

⌂⌂…17…⌂⌂

Morning cleaned the grill with a metal spatula, her bony shoulders bouncing as she leaned into her work. Otis dialed. The manager answered. Otis ordered a fried egg and bagel. He saw Morning turn and nod. She broke an egg on the grill, sliced a bagel, melted cheese. She assembled the sandwich and wrapped it in paper. The manager delivered it. Otis kept his eyes on the wraith across the street as he counted out $2.79. The manager glanced over his shoulder at Morning as he pocketed the money.

At six pm, Morning changed her shoes and slung a worn bag over her shoulder. She stood on the sidewalk in front of the café waiting for a bus. Otis closed the store. His six-year-old Toyota turned onto Harrison just as her bus turned left onto Main. He was parked in the alley behind her house when she lit the candle. He peered through the bathroom window as she pulled her long-sleeved turtleneck over her head and took out her razor. He left her resting on the cracked linoleum, four new slices weeping under yesterday's scabs. He passed another phantom headed towards Morning's apartment as he headed home.

The hunger increased. Otis closed the store the next day at noon and drove to her apartment. He slipped the lock with his MasterCard and stood in the living-bedroom, breathing her scent into his lungs. He ran a finger along the spines of her beat-up, paperback books. Her closets were empty, her drawers full. There were no photos, no letters, no address books. An unopened carton of cherry yogurt sat in the refrigerator. He rested his cheek on her small flat pillow.

He was back by one-fifteen. The lunch crowd had thinned at the café. The manager leaned a chair back on two legs against the wall and pretended to read. Morning bussed the tables. Otis strolled across the street and sat at the lunch counter. New scratches adorned the backs of her hands as she served his chilidog.

He hired a clerk to run the store on Thursdays. Morning didn't work at the coffee shop on Thursdays. The first time he followed her bus to the hospital, he lost her inside the building. That evening, she moved the purple candle into her bedroom. He waited at the bathroom window for three days before she returned to him. The next Thursday, he found her in a large room on the fourth floor of the outpatient clinic. She rocked in her seat and cried.

Each evening, Otis trembled as the razor caressed her arms, her thighs, her belly—even her breasts. He cherished those few moments of intimacy with her and the blade. Perhaps she sensed his presence, perhaps not. He owned her most private time all the same.

He learned her patterns. On hectic days, the cuts grew deeper and she dripped hot wax on them. She panted on the floor afterwards and fell into a shallow sleep. On good days, she curled on the floor beneath the sink without the blade. Once, after a blissful afternoon at a park, she wept while she ripped the top layer of skin on her foot with a hot needle. On Thursdays, she took deep breaths and muttered, "STOP!" over and over before she cut.

Captivated by her skeletal charm like a vulture drawn to a fading animal, Otis understood there would be others—predators eager to steal a morsel. He guarded his prey like a jealous lover. Often he napped in his car in the alley behind the Rhododendrons. Once he heard footsteps. He flashed the Toyota's headlights and something scuttled off through the brush. Another time, he chased a long-legged interloper away from his private chapel beneath her window with loud curses and chunks of sandstone.

One Thursday afternoon, an older woman who looked like Morning, rang Morning's bell. Otis hid behind the bus stop. Morning opened the door. Her eyes widened and her mouth formed a tight little "O." The women faced each other. Morning smiled. It burst across her face like dawn on a cloudless day. Otis had never seen her do that. She threw her arms around the woman's neck. They clung to each other as they went inside.

Otis hurried across the street. It was daytime. He didn't dare hide in the bushes. He hoisted himself up onto the roof of the neighbor's porch, grasped a thick limb of the shade tree and swung, hand over hand, until he found a secure fork near the trunk. From there, he could see into Morning's living-bedroom.

She sat cross-legged on the floor chatting with her well-dressed guest. After about twenty minutes, they stood up. The visitor threw her fur coat over her arm and collected her alligator purse. Morning took a thick sweater out of her drawer. As Morning pulled the sweater over her head, her long-sleeved t-shirt rose up from the waistband of her pants. The older woman dropped her purse. She marched over to Morning and lifted the knit shirt. She stared. She took Morning's left arm and pushed the sleeve up over the elbow. Covering her mouth with her hands, she stepped back, then lunged forward and slapped Morning. Morning pressed a palm against her reddening cheek and the joy drained from her face. The guest dashed out of the apartment. Morning followed as far as the door. She shouted something at the figure retreating down the street. Otis thought she said, "Mommy!"

It was the middle of a cloudy afternoon. There were no customers at the café. The lights in the restaurant were out. Otis glimpsed the manager leaning over Morning, his face buried in her neck. The tall man crowded her into a corner, her arms pinned to her sides. She stamped on his foot. The manager's face contorted. He stepped back and swung. Blood spurted from her nose. She grabbed her bag and hurried out of the restaurant. He called to her, but she ignored him and ran down Harrison. He sank into a booth and laughed.

Otis closed the store and drove to her apartment. He parked in the alley. The front door was open. He crept down the hallway. He stepped over her black, long-sleeved t-shirt, her ragged jeans with the flower appliqué on the knee, her loafers. He found her panties in the living-bedroom.

She soaked in the bathtub, reddish water covering her thighs. She held a knife. Scars criss-crossed her chest. Blood dripped from seven new cuts carved into her stomach. She startled when she saw him. Her flesh squeaked against enamel as she drew back.

He pierced her with his eyes.

Her face melted and she nodded. Holding the knife out to him, she said, "Help me."

He knelt beside the tub. "Are you sure?"

"It's time." A pink tear trickled down her cheek.

She was ripe—a virgin eager for consummation. Her lower lip quivered, her eyes beseeched.

He accepted the blade and stroked her cheek with the tip, opening a long red wound. She moaned. The intimacy thrilled him. He panted as he carved. Her final breath warmed his face. He stepped back to watch life gush into the bathwater. Fulfillment swept through him and he sighed. He sat down on the closed lid of the toilet.

Hungry eyes caressed the carcass from the window. Otis roared and fake charged. The phantom slunk back through the Rhododendrons. Otis paced, protecting his kill.

# YOU NEVER TAKE ME BOWLING

He spoke to me of love but he meant sex. This was just fine with me since I spoke to him of sex and meant love. A lot of people confused those two issues so I didn't feel bad about it. Lance was the latest in a long line of unpopular boys I'd given blowjobs in the parking lot behind the bowling alley. I'd meet him in his ratty old car, stick my chewing gum behind my ear, unzip his Bugle Boys and get down to it right away. At the important moment, he would scream out his love for me. That was all I ever asked.

That's why I was surprised to find a perky little bow tied to his equipment one rainy afternoon. It made him look like a swollen Vienna sausage cinched at the top with purple grosgrain ribbon. I wasn't sure what I was supposed to do next. No one had bothered to gift-wrap it before. Should I untie it? Or simply do my business with the bow in place? "Okay, what's the deal here?" I sat up, focused on the fuzzy red dice hanging from his rearview mirror, and straightened my blouse. Changes in routine threw me.

"Awww, come on, Emmeline. I thought you'd like it." Lance held himself in one hand and jiggled it around." Aren't you even curious about what's under the bow?"

"I've SEEN what's under that bow twenty-two times." I slipped the wad of Double Bubble back in my mouth and rolled my eyes.

He cranked down the window and peered into the outside mirror like he was expecting someone. "Twenty-three. Don't forget the time we did it under the blanket at the drive-in."

"We never 'did it.' I'm a virgin." I took a joint out of my purse and lit it. Inhaling deeply, I held it in my lungs as long as I could.

"You know what I mean." Lance jiggled himself once more. "Just pull the string, baby."

I pulled on the loose ribbon and the elaborate bow disintegrated to reveal a key tied under it. "What's this?" I held it up, a couple yards of purple ribbon dangling below it.

"The key to heaven." Lance pointed to the number 42 stamped in the metal. "And that's our lucky number."

"I ain't going to no motel with you, Lance McCoy." I sucked hard on my joint. I didn't like where this was going.

"Don't you get tired of doing the same old thing every time?" His voice got deeper, softer. "Besides, you're my girlfriend. Don't you want to please me?" I blew smoke out my nose and glanced at him. He was half my size—he was a little too skinny and I was a lot too fat. He had picked the pimples on his forehead until they were inflamed and oozing. He wasn't much of a bargain, but he was the best I could do. Even he wouldn't spend twenty minutes alone with me if it weren't for the blowjob.

"I'm not your girlfriend. Since when did you ever take me anywhere but here?" I gestured to the dumpster sitting by the backdoor of the bowling alley.

"I took you to the drive-in." He took the joint out of my hand and puffed quickly.

"You take me places where no one will see us. You never take me bowling or out to Denny's or to your friends." Of course, I wasn't sure he had that many friends anyway.

"I didn't know you liked to bowl." I almost believed that fact raised me in his estimation. "I've never seen you inside."

"No one ever takes me inside." I took my joint away from him and scowled. If he hadn't started this bullshit, we'd be done by now and I'd be walking home in the rain. We both knew that.

"Come to the motel with me, Emmie. I promise I'll take you bowling the next time we get together. I'll even spring for a couple of big Macs one of these days."

"Don't do me any favors." My nose burned like I was going to cry.

He rubbed the fog off the windshield with his sleeve and squinted into the mist. "I haven't told you this before, but I think you are beautiful," he said as if his mind was elsewhere. He straightened himself and zipped his pants before leaning over to kiss my cheek. He smelled like stale Doritos. It was the first time he ever kissed me.

"HA! Don't give me that." I was down to the roach and was beginning to feel smudgy around the edges. "You're sweet on Lynette Johnson. I've seen you mooning around her."

"Get out! Lynnette ain't going to notice the likes of me." His cheeks darkened. It may have been a blush but I wasn't sure. Maybe it was the reflection from the neon lights across the street. He glanced at his watch like he was on a schedule. "Please?" He struggled to start the car. It moaned in protest as he ground the ignition. I slipped the rest of the roach into a baggie and tucked it into my purse. "Please, Emmie?"

I took a deep breath and nodded. It wasn't like I chose to protect my virginity. No one ever wanted it before. I was cautiously excited.

The engine finally caught and he gunned it several times. He pulled out of the parking lot and headed towards town. The windshield wipers hypnotized me. A guy once slipped his hand inside my bra, but I'd never been naked in front of anyone before. The thought made me a little queasy. Maybe I could turn out the lights and crawl into bed while he was in the bathroom or something. Would it hurt when he stuck it in me? Lance wasn't as big as some of the other guys I'd known, but he was big enough. I wondered if he'd done it before. I doubted it considering he was a couple years younger than me and kinda goofy-looking. I chewed the side of my thumbnail. I liked blowjobs. I was in charge as long as I had him in my mouth. Heck, I could bite the whole thing off if he gave me any lip. This was a whole different ballgame.

"I changed my mind."

Lance drove on as if I hadn't spoken. Finally, he took a deep breath. "You can trust me." He took my hand—another first. "You know how much I love you."

I didn't believe he loved me, but it was nice to pretend someone did.

He turned into the drive of the Downtowner Motel and parked at the far end. He touched my hair. One of his eyes was blue and the other brown. I'd never noticed before. The left one twitched. It wasn't that I loved him. In fact, he kinda creeped me out—but

Lance was the only one who ever asked. How could I say no? We got out of the car and ran through the rain. I towered over him, my thighs whispering against each other with every step.

At room 42, he used the key. Mildew and bleach and other people's dust coated us as we entered. I squeezed into the tiny bathroom. The door didn't close tightly and I worried he would hear if I used the toilet. I splashed water on my face and used a washcloth under my arms and between my legs. I stuck my chewing gum behind my ear. I was almost ready when someone knocked on the outside door.

It was still raining when I woke. The lights in the cheap room burned yellow. I was afraid to move, afraid they'd come after me again. I watched them through swollen slits, trying not to cry. The sheets under me were soaked with blood and semen and urine.

Lance sat on the floor counting the money from my purse. "Twelve dollars and twenty-two cents," he announced.

"Damn bitch." A bare-chested, pot-bellied man kicked the bed, jostling me, and jerked the three bills from Lance's outstretched hand. "You could have found someone a lot richer, baby boy—or a lot better looking."

"She was the best I could do, Bubba." Lance's voice was so tight it squeaked. "I'm not up to my neck in cheerleaders you know." He tossed him my stash.

Bubba held the baggie in his palm, judging the weight. There wasn't much there. "I did get a good laugh watching you mount her, though. Was like a Chihuahua taking an elephant." He scratched his testicles before ripping the hoops from my lobes. I squealed and covered my ear with my hand. "Shut up, slut!" I glimpsed his hairy knuckles a moment before his fist connected with my jaw. I choked on my own blood but I didn't whimper.

"All right. That's enough. We are even. Get out of here!" Lance kicked at the man's brogans, scowling. Something about Lance's anger got to me. After all, where was he before?

"The little dawg's got a temper, does he?" The man mussed Lance's greasy hair, then wiped his palm on the seat of his pants and grimaced.

"You got what you wanted. It's over."

"Oh, it ain't over, kid. You think a fat broad and some trinkets puts us even? This is just the first payment." Bubba stuffed my jewelry into his back pocket. "And if I want to give this whore another lick, ain't nothing you can do about it." He stood over Lance, his fists clenched.

I rose up on one elbow. Lance was no match for Bubba. I grabbed hold of the metal lamp on the nightstand. It was glued down. Why anyone would want this crap I couldn't guess, but everything that could be stolen was nailed down. Bubba continued to threaten Lance who cowered in the corner, but he pointed at me and bellowed. "YOU! Lay back down there and spread your legs."

That was it. I struggled to my feet. Embarrassed by my body, I fumbled for my t-shirt. I tried to get it over my head, but Bubba turned away from Lance and jerked it out of my hands.

"Did you hear me?" He had probably been good-looking twenty years ago. His thick lips turned downwards. "Did you hear me, bitch!"

I put all my weight into a punch that caught Bubba just under the chin. My fingers stung, but the look of surprise on his face was worth it. Shrieking at him, I charged. He backed away—and I realized he was afraid of me. He snapped me with my t-shirt, first on my chest, then in my face. I kicked at his knees and he dodged me, ducking under my arm. I whirled, ready to pummel him, just as he ran out the door with my shirt in his hand.

I locked the door behind him and went to the bathroom, leaving Lance cowering in the corner. Sitting on the toilet, I dabbed at myself with toilet paper. It came away bloody.

"Emmeline?"

"Go away, Lance!" I pulled on my panties and jeans, put on my bra. Taking a deep breath, I looked in the mirror. How would I explain the bruises to my Grandma? What would the kids at school think? I splashed water over my face.

"I'm sorry, Emmie." Lance tapped on the door. "I owed him something. You understand?"

"Go away," I shouted.

"You'll be alright."

I threw open the door and it hit him before he could back away. "Leave me alone," I said. Bubba had taken my top. I rummaged around the room looking for something to wear. I found Bubba's green work shirt wadded at the foot of the bed. It had 'Bubba' embroidered over the chest pocket—'Lawson Trucking' arced across the back. It was too small for me. I left with the stained sheet clutched to my chest, the shirt tossed over my shoulders.

Lance trailed along behind me with my purse in his hands. "I'll take you home."

"Since when?" I picked up my pace. Cold raindrops pounded us. Goosebumps covered my arms.

"Get in the truck, will ya?"

"NO!"

"Don't be that way, Emmeline."

I turned and threw the work shirt in his face.

"YOU GET INSIDE DRESSED LIKE THAT, YOUNG LADY!" A cop driving the other way yelled out his window as he sped by. I looked around. Home was blocks away, I was half-naked and it was raining.

"The city doesn't take too kindly to a girl walking down the street in her brassiere and a dirty sheet." Lance took my arm and led me back to the pickup. We were both soaked and shivering.

"I could go to the cops. I could give them Bubba's shirt," I said as I crawled up into the truck.

"But you won't." He closed the door. "You came with me to that room. You said I could have you."

His cockiness made me boil. "I didn't say Bubba could have me. I didn't say you could rob me." We sat in the truck. The windows fogged up almost immediately.

"You live in a big house. I thought you'd have money."

"HA! Fooled you." I took my compact out of my purse and flipped it open. My left cheekbone hurt. I touched it with the tips of my fingers.

"Looks like you got a black eye."

"Ain't anyone going to hit me ever again."

"I didn't hit you."

"You might as well have."

He started the engine. "You don't understand."

"No, I don't. I don't want to."

"Nothing ever works out for me." He rubbed the windshield with his elbow. "Whatever I touch turns to shit."

"Poor baby!"

"Don't be that way, Emmeline." He backed out of the parking lot and headed down Towson. "We didn't take nothing you needed." He drove past Lawson's Trucking. I twisted in my seat and noted the address.

"I'll be anyway I please." I'd go after them both, I fantasized. I'd make them pay. I'd hurt them like they hurt me. Somehow.

"So, Emmeline. You still want to go bowling?"

# SIMON SAYS

*The song ended. Amplified static hissed in his ears. The bed squeaked as he straddled her. The thrashing branches of the chestnut trees outside the window blended with Simon's voice. "Do it."*

🏠🏘️

Twenty round tables with elaborate center pieces clustered around the small dance floor. As the French doors from the lobby swung open, the band played a two-bar flourish.

🏠🏘️...44...🏘️🏠

"Surprise!" Two hundred people in formal attire rose to their feet and applauded. Paul stood in the threshold with his wife Linda on his arm.

"You did this." He smiled into her eyes.

She took a white rose boutonnière from a silver tray proffered by the Club Manager and pinned it to his lapel. "We couldn't let your big day come and go without notice." She stood on tiptoe to kiss his cheek.

"I'll deal with you later." He squeezed her hand.

"Happy Birthday, Paul." A burley man clapped him on the back.

"Harvey." Paul acknowledged his brother-in-law with a hearty handshake. The band broke into an old Doors' tune, 'Break on through to the Other Side.'

Harvey gestured toward a table near the front where three middle-aged men stood grinning. "Linda tracked down everyone."

"I can't believe it." Paul waved at his fraternity brothers as Linda guided him to his position in the receiving line. "You must have been working on this for months."

"Oh she has. You can't say my sister isn't a go getter." Harvey put his arm around Linda's shoulders.

"And beautiful too."

"It's time, Paul." She touched his cheek.

"I know."

*She lay beneath him like white stone, unmoving save for the pulse throbbing in her neck. Her blouse was ripped open. The buttons lay scattered on the floor beside the bed. He licked his lips. Someone lifted the needle and moved it to the beginning of the album. Rock music filled the room.*

...46...

The rest of the guests left just after ten. Paul threw Linda a kiss before she closed the French doors behind her.

"To the man of the hour!" The medals on Billy Rex's uniform rattled as he lifted his martini.

"Here, here." Reggie retained a hint of his English boarding school accent.

Paul took off his jacket and hung it on the back of the chair Reggie offered him. "It's great to see you guys."

"Now the REAL party begins." Harvey gestured to the waiter who scurried over. "Another round."

"Yes sir." The boy's manner was ostentatious and the men snickered.

"Whew. That's a bit much." Billy Rex fanned himself with both hands and rolled his eyes.

"What was it that Simon used to call guys like that?" Reggie gestured toward the retreating figure.

"Mollies." Roger ran a finger under his thin starched collar where it cut into his neck.

"No, it was Miss Mollies." Harvey took off his coat too—and loosened his bowtie.

"I hope we weren't such arrogant little wimps in our day." Roger popped an antacid.

"We were worse, I'm afraid." Paul passed a box of Cuban cigars around the table. "We didn't have to work in a private club for fat cats like us."

"I was too stupid to know how lucky we were." Billy Rex selected a cigar and tucked it into the breast pocket of his jacket. "I was nearly fifty before it struck me."

"Simon was the only one to appreciate our advantages back then." Paul bit the end off of his cigar and spit onto a cut-glass ashtray. "He used to say that we were weaned to caviar instead of pablum."

"I sometimes wonder where we would be had he lived." Harvey accepted the cigar box from Reggie and slid it across the table to Paul.

"In prison." Reggie's laugh echoed in the room now that the band was gone. The other men fell silent.

"What?" Reggie raised his brows but the others refused to look at him.

*"She wanted it. She came here to get it." Harvey backed into a dark corner, fumbling with his pants.*

*"Who is she?" Paul crouched over her, his beery breath lifting her bangs.*

*"What does it matter? She's a slut." Roger belched and tightened his grip on her arm. "Take your turn or back off and give the rest of us a shot."*

...49...

"What the hell happened to this party?" Reggie broke the silence. "I thought we were here to celebrate the senator-elect's birthday."

"It's been thirty-five years. That one night is the only thing that links us now." Billy Rex stirred his martini with his pinkie. "That and Simon."

"Did you know I went to grade school with him?" Paul leaned back in his chair and lit his cigar with a match. "We went back that far."

"Always the practical joker—and competitive! That boy loved to win." Roger's wheezy laugh turned into a cough. "Remember the time Reggie cut him off in a footrace?"

"Oh yes, I thought he was going to pop a blood vessel," Reggie said. "Such a big stink over nothing."

"He expected a lot of himself." Paul dipped the unlit end of his cigar into his scotch. "His father was a self-made man. Built that business from nothing. Simon had to live up to that."

Harvey set a briefcase on the table. "It was grades. That was where he excelled. Straight A's as long as I can remember."

🏠🏛🏘

*Her body was fleshy—one breast larger than the other. Paul unzipped his pants and jerked her thighs open. Her eyes stopped him. He loomed over her, unsure what to do until her hatred withered him. He glanced over his shoulder. Harvey watched—his mouth agape with post-coital exhaustion. Simon folded his arms over his chest. "Do it."*

🏠🏛🏘

The waiter collected their empty glasses. "Anything else, General?"

The corners of Billy Rex's mouth quivered. "Not yet."

"How about you, Father?"

"No thank you, young man." Roger belched behind his fist as the boy hurried back to his post in the bar across the room.

"Nothing's changed except your belches smell like bourbon instead of beer." Billy Rex held his nose.

"Sorry." Roger burped again, gripping the wooden crucifix he wore around his neck.

"Simon had a way with women, didn't he?" Paul glanced from face to face, assessing the effect his non-sequitur had on his guests.

"Well, yes. He had the knack." Reggie avoided Paul's eyes.

"So what did he have against that one?" Harvey took a leather agenda out of his briefcase along with a gold Cross pen.

Silence.

Paul puffed on his cigar. Roger's response was subtle—just a tightening around his mouth, the finger inside the cleric's collar again.

"Man, oh man." Billy Rex ran his hand over his military-short gray hair.

"Is this why we are here?" Reggie set his drink on the table. "I spent a lifetime trying to forget and you want to rehash it? Why?"

"Because I saw her," Harvey said. "I talked to her."

*"Get outta my way." Reggie pushed him aside and climbed onto the bed. Paul backed away, embarrassed by his failure in front of the guys.*

*The girl struggled, scratching Roger's face. "If you aren't going to do it, at least hold her down for the rest of us."*

*Tears ran down her cheeks. "Help me," she mouthed.*

...53...

*"I can't," Paul said as he gripped her free wrist.*

Reggie knocked over his chair as he stood. "Jesus, Harvey. Why would you do such a thing? That little slut could ruin us. She could file charges. Think what she could do to Paul's new career."

"There's a statute of limitations on rape," Billy Rex burst out. "No one's going to arrest us after all this time."

"I asked him to find her, Reggie." Paul's cigar smoke floated over their heads. "I couldn't stop thinking about her—about us, about what we did. Besides, I couldn't take the chance of her surfacing during the campaign."

"Was she okay?" Roger folded his hands on the table and lowered his eyes.

"I suppose so. Turns out, she's a very successful woman."

"Thank God for that." Roger's voice turned gruff and he put a trembling hand over his eyes.

"We didn't even know her name," Billy Rex said.

Harvey slipped on a pair of reading glasses and paged through his agenda. "She wasn't that hard to find. I used the firm's investigator. He made a few inquiries and we had her name inside of a week."

*He was careful to avoid her nails. The scratch on Roger's face oozed blood. Reggie was a big boy. He put a massive hand over her mouth while he raped her. Roger covered her face with a pillow case when it was his turn. They turned her over and Billy Rex took her from behind. Her screams became howls.*

*Paul glanced at Simon. His smile had faded.*

*The music blared.*

...55...

"So what did she say? Did she give us absolution?" Reggie paced. "Did she forgive us?"

Harvey peered at Reggie over the top of his glasses. "There are some things that are unforgivable. She hates our guts. What do you think?"

"I don't know. I kind of hoped, you know. Prayed."

"Hoped for what?"

Reggie avoided Harvey's eyes. "That I'd forget even if she didn't, that I'd never see her again."

Roger sighed and rubbed his belly. "Every year, I tell myself that I'm not like that—that I couldn't have done what I did. I keep expecting to be punished, but no police officer ever shows up at my door. I pray for that girl every time I say Mass. I go to confession—but I can't say enough 'Hail Marys' to make the sick feeling in my stomach go away. Every little disappointment, every small misfortune—I think, this is it. Yet when it's all over and things return to normal, I know I still haven't been punished enough."

Paul nodded. "When my daughters were born, I couldn't help but worry that someone would do to them what we did to that kid. That's what she was, you know—a kid barely seventeen. I became obsessed with protecting my girls. That's why I went to law school—why I became a prosecutor—so I could put away jackasses like us."

Billy Rex motioned to the waiter who lounged behind the bar. "Anybody else want another drink?"

"I've had more than enough to drink, Billy." Roger chased another pill with the last of his bourbon.

"When did you last get a check-up?" Reggie knelt beside Roger, pinched his chin between his thumb and forefinger, and turned his bloated face first one way and then the other.

Roger grimaced and pulled away. "Once a year. Insurance, you know."

Reggie stood up and tossed a business card on the table in front of Roger. "Have your internist call me. Sooner or later you are going to need surgery."

"How the hell would you know that?" Billy Rex snorted.

"I know because it's my job to know." Reggie spun around, scowling. "I do three surgeries a day. I'm board certified in three specialties. I've written two books."

"I don't need your résumé." Billy Rex hit the table with his fist, knocking over his empty glass.

"Okay, okay. Enough." Paul raised his voice. "Can't you two spend one evening together without getting on each other's nerves?"

"Some people never change." Billy Rex sniffed.

Reggie laughed. "Oh, that hurt."

"Twenty lashes with a wet noodle, as Simon used to say," Harvey muttered under his breath.

The waiter brought Billy Rex a fresh martini. He fluttered his eyelashes, but Billy was no longer in the mood to flirt. He took a sip and smacked his lips. "Sometimes at night, I wake up thinking that I can hear her screaming. It's like she's a ghost or something, haunting me. I haven't touched a woman since then."

This confession surprised no one. Paul guessed that she was the ONLY woman Billy ever touched.

"All this guilt is unbecoming. Do what I did, for crying out loud. Don't think about it. Don't stir things up. Move on." Reggie dug into the pockets of his tux trousers and dropped wadded up hundred dollar bills on the table. "Here. Pay her off."

Billy Rex clenched his fist, the muscles in his jaw twitching.

"I tried that. She's got money. Ours doesn't interest her." Harvey shook his head. "I wish it was that simple."

Paul flicked a long ash off his cigar. "I tried using money to get rid of the guilt when I started that foundation to build safe houses for abused women. It was Linda's idea, of course, but I bought into it all the way. It was a good thing for the women but it didn't help how I felt. Nothing does."

"My God, Paul. You told Linda?" Reggie threw up his hands. "I thought we promised each other we'd never tell anyone what we did."

"Actually, I didn't tell her until Harvey came back from Alabama. We told her together."

Harvey bowed his head. "All these years, I dreaded the thought of my family knowing what I did. My parents are dead now, so they were spared that shame—but telling Linda was worse than I could imagine. She's my baby sister. She looked up to me."

Billy Rex placed his hand on Harvey's shoulder. "Linda knows you, Harvey. My God, look at all the things you've done over the years. You created half the jobs available in this city. You rebuilt Old Town. I'm sure she still looks up to you."

"There's a difference between sticking with you and forgiveness." Paul blew smoke through his nostrils. "She still loves us, if that's what you mean—but she knows we behaved like animals."

"Before we told her, I knew I wasn't the man she thought I was." Harvey's voice rasped as though he was nearly out of air. "Now she knows it too."

Reggie folded his arms over his chest and looked down on the others. "That's what I mean. Why tell her? Why hurt her that way?"

"I couldn't stand her not knowing." Paul said softly. "Perhaps it was like Roger's urge to confess. I spent the last thirty-five years trying to make up for it. A lifetime of trying to do the right thing—maybe trying too hard. Perhaps Linda's knowing what we did is my punishment."

"The worst punishment of all." Harvey muttered.

*"STOP! Stop!" Simon grabbed Billy Rex and pulled him away from the girl. She lay*

*face down on the bed, sobbing. Roger and Paul released her arms and stood up.*

*The sound of Billy's zipper ripped the air. Harvey ran for the door, tripping over the girl's shoes.*

*"Go on. Get out." Simon gestured with his head. Billy Rex pushed Reggie out of the way and stormed out into the hallway.*

"Candace Markham." Harvey tapped a page in his agenda with his pen. "Her name was Candace. She was a scholarship student. Even though she was two years younger than us, she was in one of Simon's honors classes."

"Honor?" Roger's coughing fit lasted a long time.

"Why are we here?" Reggie sat down, drumming his fingers on the table. "What did she want?"

"I didn't remember that she was pretty." Harvey started. "Maybe she wasn't then, but she is now. She's tiny. I towered over her when she stood to shake my hand as I introduced myself. Turns out, she didn't know our names either—except for Simon, of course."

"Did you tell her how sorry we are?" Billy Rex kept his military bearing, his chin high.

"How sorry are we?" Reggie sighed. "It was a gang-bang, for God's sake. Beneath us? Certainly. Naughty? Definitely. Stupid? You bet. But what was Miss Markham doing in our frat house anyway? Doesn't she have to bear some of the responsibility? A good girl wouldn't have been lolling around in Simon's bed—drunk on God knows what."

Billy Rex glared at Reggie. "Do you really think she wanted us to do that to her?"

"Stop it, now. Both of you." Paul stubbed out his cigar. "Let's just leave it that it bothered some of us more than others, okay? Let Harvey finish."

"Sorry, Harvey." Billy Rex gave a quick two-fingered salute.

"Anyway, when I met Miss Markham, I explained who I was and she asked me to sit down. Considering the circumstances, she was hospitable. She didn't know me. She knew of Paul, of course—because of the campaign, but she never realized he took part in the attack. I'm sure she knows who you are, Billy Rex, after all those press conferences you held during the last war. Don't worry, I didn't tell her you were one of us. I was there to discuss my role—and Paul's."

"I appreciate that. The Army would not understand."

"I asked her what we could do for her," Harvey continued. "She stared at me a long time—trying to figure out why I'd come, I guess. Finally she told me that she wanted nothing from us. She wasn't going to destroy anyone's reputation. Not because she felt a thing for us—we didn't deserve her consideration—but she had a daughter and a mother. She didn't want them put through the brouhaha an accusation would cause."

"So see, it was a useless trip. She's forgotten all about it." Reggie gathered up the money he'd tossed on the table and smoothed out the bills.

"Not forgotten. She wanted to know if Simon said anything before he hung himself, if he left a message."

Roger's eyes clung to the money. "What did you tell her?"

"I told her what he wrote."

Reggie shrugged and pushed the stack of bills across the table toward the priest. "Not much of a consolation since no one knows what he meant."

"She knew. It was something they were discussing in one of their classes."

"What was that?" Roger thumbed through the money, folded it, and stuck it in his pocket.

Paul took a deep breath. "Betrayal."

*The others left. One by one, the doors to their rooms clicked shut. The girl moaned and felt around for her panties.*

*"Let me help you," Simon said.*

*She jerked her arm away.*

*"I didn't know I had that power." He rummaged in his chest of drawers, finding one of his shirts. "Here wear this."*

*The shirt hung almost to her knees. At the base of her skull, her hair was matted and tangled. A bruise was forming on her forehead. Paul didn't believe anyone had hit her. Maybe she'd bumped it against the head of the bed?*

Simon knelt to pick up her shoes. "I can understand your anger, but don't be afraid. I won't hurt you."

She swung with all her might, her fist connecting under Simon's chin since he was bent over. Her shoes flew out of his hand. He staggered back against the wall and slid to the floor.

"You bitch!" He winced and cupped his hand over his chin. "You made me bite my tongue."

Paul handed her a fringed purse. "Do you want me to drive you home?"

"I'd die before I let you do anything for me." Her bare feet made smacking sounds on the tile of the hallway as she ran toward the stairs.

"Okay, so it was something between her and Simon. He's dead. It's over and done with," Reggie said.

"She did want to know one thing." Paul held up his forefinger. "Harvey and I have discussed it at length."

"She wanted to know why, didn't she?" Roger asked. "She wanted to know why we did it."

Paul's eyes rested on the priest. Roger looked older than the rest of them. The years spent working in the ghettos had worn him down—too many nights trudging through the cold streets looking for people needing shelter, too many funeral masses for drug addicts and AIDS patients, not enough baptisms or confirmations or weddings.

Harvey glanced at Paul. "We were kids. We all adored Simon. We were stupid. I've wondered about it every day of my life. Here we are—successful people. All of us are in leadership positions, yet back then we allowed a boy so weak-willed that he gave up on life before he could vote to dictate what we had for dinner."

Reggie snorted. "Simon was a little Churchill. He had the gift of gab. Any kind of garbage coming out of his mouth sounded like a good idea."

Billy Rex gazed at the good-looking waiter working behind the bar. "He knew our weaknesses and played on them. He told me I should go into the military because that's where one finds thousands of boys willing to obey without question."

Reggie chuckled. "He told me that surgery was the perfect career for someone who couldn't tell the difference between a person and a steak. It's downright insulting now, but at the time I thought it was charming."

"So the gist here is that we obeyed him because we liked his way with words?" Paul scratched his head.

"Maybe Simon had nothing to do with our big sin. Did you ever think that maybe we did it because we were immoral little bastards who took advantage of the situation?"

They stared at Reggie with horror.

*Paul knelt beside Simon. "Are you hurt?"*

*"Hell yeah." He rubbed his chin.*

*"You think she'll call the police?"*

*"Naw, she'll just go home."*

*"You think she's okay?"*

*"Relax, Paul. She's fine. You know what they say about sin."*

*"No, what do they say?" Paul slipped his arm around Simon's back and helped him up.*

*"It'll sink a ship."*

*"You aren't making any sense. You are drunk."*

*"I can't believe they did it. It was magnificent. They were like sheep. They didn't ask a single question—not even you."*

*"I can't believe it either."* Paul put Simon to bed, covering him with a bloodstained sheet.

*"I fixed her wagon, Paul. I showed her."*

*"Yes, I know."*

*"I won't be shown up. Not by the likes of her."*

*"No, you won't."* Paul turned out the overhead lights as he left.

***

"There are all kinds of answers for what we did." Roger's knees cracked as he stood up. "None of them are satisfactory. I'm supposed to teach redemption. Perhaps, the price of salvation is never-ending guilt. I don't know." He shook Paul's hand. "Good luck, Senator. Use what you know well."

"Thank you, Father." Paul slipped a few more dollars into Roger's hand. Paul knew the money would be well-spent.

The heavy-set priest smiled. The dimple in his cheek reminded Paul of the boy Roger had been. Roger turned to Reggie who was still seated at the table by Billy Rex and mouthed the words, "Thank you."

Reggie blushed and waved him away. After Roger left, Reggie turned on his pager. "Is that why you wanted to see us, Senator?"

"Maybe I just wanted to see an old friend."

"Don't give me that. You are a liberal Democrat. You wanted to fix the unfixable. What's past is past, Paul. You can't change it."

"Thanks for coming, Doctor."

Billy Rex waited until the French doors closed behind Reggie. "I admired

Simon. He was popular and funny. I wanted to be like him. I thought if I hung out with him, dressed like him, talked like him—if I did what he did, that maybe the magic would wear off. I was wrong. We all were."

"Look at you, General. You are a hero. There's not a little boy in the country that doesn't want to be like you. You made your own magic."

"It's a house of cards, Paul. It could come crashing down around my ears at any moment." Billy Rex put on his hat and squared his shoulders.

"Perhaps you tried so hard because of Simon."

"Perhaps we all tried so hard because of Candace." Billy gestured with his eyes toward the bar. "I have a little business to conduct. Do you mind?"

Paul glanced at the boy leaning against the bar. "No, of course not. It was good to see you, Billy Rex."

Billy marched across the room.

Paul shook his head. "Well, Harvey, you never did get around to asking them about the girl."

Harvey closed his book and took off his glasses. "Whoever set up that account for Candace doesn't want us or her to know. We gave him plenty of opportunity to speak up but he chose silence. Asking would have been useless."

"So who do you think it is?"

"They are all good guys. Could be any of them."

"Will Candace accept that her benefactor doesn't want to be identified?"

"I'm sure she will."

"Why do you think she wants to know so much?"

"She told me she was going to throw the money in his face."

***

*The door was unlatched. Paul pushed it open with his elbow. At first he didn't see Simon hanging in the shower. His eyes went to the window over Simon's bed. Someone had written on it with the girl's blood red lipstick.*

> *'Under the spreading chestnut tree,*
> *I sold you and you sold me:*
> *There lie they and here lie we,*
> *Under the spreading chestnut tree.'*

# GOD BLESS THE SINNER

My mother was Southern Baptist, my father a drunk. I grew up in a violently virtuous home. But now, I embrace sin. I'm a big believer in it. When I'm alone and in the dark, it's the only thing that makes me feel whole. Before I began my little projects, I was little more than a Xerox copy of a blank sheet of paper—warm nothingness. But sin

...77...

colored me with a 48-box of Crayola Crayons and I have been redeemed.

Looking back, I realize it began in May of 1956 when I was thirteen. The old man passed out on the couch while Mom pelted him with Fritos and intoned ominous biblical warnings. I grabbed a warm Pepsi and pinched one of her Pall Malls on my way out the back door. I could still hear her squawking, "Rod? Rod!" when I turned the corner half a block from our house. I leaned against the streetlight and sucked on the cigarette. A shadow flickered across a shade in the yellow house on the corner of Elm Street. I blew smoke out my nose and stared, transfixed.

My fourth grade teacher, Mrs. Thompson, lived there. I stepped over the low picket fence and hid behind a shrub. The window wasn't quite closed. She leaned over the tub, her tits dangling, her white-streaked belly bulging. The hairy patch between her legs was brillo-pad gray. So was her old-lady hairdo. She'd already washed her face so she didn't have eyebrows. I unzipped my fly and stroked my baby cock while I watched her bathe. It's my favorite memory from childhood.

By the time I was seventeen, I spent most nights roaming the neighborhood peeking at dozens of women. By nineteen, watching wasn't enough. I lay in bed at night and dreamed about hunting, pouncing. The image of fearful eyes aroused me and I grunted with pleasure as I masturbated.

I made my first attempt at twenty, creeping up behind a fleshy woman loading groceries into the trunk of her car. I split her scalp with a crow bar, but had to leave her when a truck turned into the parking lot. I ran like hell, terrified someone might have seen me. I got home late, sweaty and pissed at myself. I sucked down some of the old man's scotch and felt a little better. I was disappointed I didn't get to rape her, but seeing the news report excited me and I jacked off into my bloody t-shirt while my parents argued about Jesus in the living room.

Over the next several months, I made four less than satisfying attempts at rape. Each time, I lost my nerve and ran off at the last moment. I lost weight, I couldn't sleep. I wanted—I wanted so much. My mother's Sunday School class prayed for me. My father gave me a beer.

I discovered *The Scam* when my cousin Buddy got his girlfriend pregnant. He came by to borrow $200 from the old man. That was a lot of money in those days. Curiosity got the better of me and I followed him down the street, asking questions.

"Will you give it up?" he asked pushing me aside.

"I don't see why you won't tell me."

"I don't see why you are so curious."

"You never borrowed money before, it must be something big. You buying a car?"

"I wish," he shrugged. "But I got me a little problem I gotta settle."

"You're gambling?" My voice broke with excitement.

"I knocked Sheila up." He hitched his khakis an inch or two and rubbed his nose on the sleeve of his madras shirt.

I laughed and clapped him on the back. "You sorry, sonofabitch!" I was impressed. I'd never known anyone my age that actually got someone pregnant. The thought of just taking a girl out and asking for it intrigued me.

"Ain't nothing wrong with MY pecker." Buddy squared his shoulders and sniffed.

"A regular Don Juan." I elbowed him.

"Yeah, yeah. But now I gotta take care of it."

"How you going to do that? Your part is over."

"For crying out loud, Rod. YOU know." He arched one eyebrow. "We got a line on a doctor who does it for $200."

It? Oh—'it'! "How does it work?" I trailed along behind him. "I thought it was illegal."

"We call a number and tell who ever answers we have the money. Then someone gives Sheila an address. Probably some rented room somewhere. She's supposed to go there by herself. When she gets there, she puts on a blindfold. Someone shows up and takes the money. Then they lead her off and put her on the table and do it. After they are gone, she takes off the blindfold and goes home."

"Just like that?"

"That's it. She never sees them."

This was very interesting. "Where do you get the number?"

"She got it from a girlfriend who got it from a bulletin board over at the University. She says there are numbers floating around all over that school."

"Hell of a note." I scratched my chin, pondering. Could it really be that easy?

Buddy rubbed his fingers through his blonde crewcut. "I gotta get going, partner. She wants to get this taken care of tonight."

"Good luck, man." I stuffed my hands in the pockets of my chinos and watched him saunter off down the street towards Sheila's neighborhood. I knew exactly where she lived. I peeked at her on Tuesdays and Fridays when her parents took square dancing lessons. She had rosy little nipples and peach fuzz between her thighs. I closed my eyes and imagined her flat stomach swelled taut like a basketball. My cock twitched. I decided to follow him.

They were sitting in a glider on Sheila's front porch when I crept up behind them. She nestled her head in the crook of Buddy's shoulder. It didn't seem fair. This bastard had a good-looking girl who spread her legs for him. And he was ordinary—just an ordinary guy! I had no one but my battling parents and a bunch of strange women who didn't know I watched them.

He kissed the top of her head. Her stiff petticoat rustled as she stood up, smoothing her skirt.

"Where are you going?" he asked her as he handed her the cash.

"He said the Shangri-La Apartments. Number 25."

"I'll come for you if you take too long," he said.

"I'll be fine." She smoothed her long flip and threw a thin white cardigan over her shoulders, clipping it together over her bosom with a silver sweater chain.

I backed away and headed for the Shangri-la. I have long legs. I made it ten minutes before she did. I tiptoed into the unlocked apartment. The back bedroom door was closed. I tapped on it gently. "She's changed her mind," I called. "She couldn't get the money."

Someone inside grunted. I walked away, my loafers thumping against the hardwood floor. In the front hall, I slipped off my shoes and tiptoed into the kitchen to unbolt the back door. Then I ran out the front way, slamming the screen behind me. Hiding in the stairwell above Number 25, I waited. A minute later, Doc Lawless slipped out of the apartment, locking it behind him. He strolled out to his black Edsel, a folding table under one arm, clutching his instrument bag. He put everything in the trunk and drove away, passing Sheila as she hurried towards the Shangri-la.

I let myself in the back way. As I unlatched the front door, I heard her start up the stairs. Backing away, I hid in the bedroom and waited until she entered the apartment.

"I'm ready," she said after a moment. It sounded like a question.

I opened the door. She fidgeted in the middle of the living room wearing a white scarf around her eyes, her thin arms crossed over her chest. I unzipped my trousers and my cock sprang free.

"I left the money on the kitchen counter." She pointed.

I came up behind her and touched her shoulders. She drew back in alarm. "There, there," I whispered and she relaxed. I guided her into the bedroom.

"Should I take off my clothes?" she asked.

"Yes." I watched as she unhooked her sweater guard, stepped out of her flats, and unzipped her dress. Suddenly she was standing there in a strapless bra and slip. I wished for the table Doc Lawless took with him as I pushed her gently down on the floor. She wriggled out of her petticoat and panties.

"Now what?" The scarf covered most of her face. The nylon fluttered in and out over her nose and mouth.

"Open your legs." It was that simple. Oh, she squealed when I mounted her, but I just put my hands around her neck and squeezed. I came as she died. It was exquisite. It was better than knowing God, I WAS God. I tucked her panties—and the money—into my pocket just before leaving. I was half way down the steps when I remembered fingerprints. I went back and wiped everything down with her panties. I couldn't resist looking in on her.

She lay spread eagled—naked except for her bra—and the blindfold. The little bow above her bangs was crooked. I straightened it and then pulled the bra down so I could see her nipples. They seemed bigger than I remembered. I pressed the tiny buttons inward with my index finger. They popped right back out. Ha! I yanked the scarf away from her eyes. They were bigger than I remembered too. I felt enormous affection for her—so I gave her another go. I thought of my mother as I thrust again and again into the corpse. She'd call this sin, I realized.

And then, I was awakened, there in the Shangri-la. It was sin I'd been seeking.

Life without sin was dull and lonely. With sin, it was shiny and powerful. I became a disciple for sin as I ejaculated into Sheila's pretty little body.

The next day I tacked a small sign on a bulletin board in the Student Union of a small college in the next town. "Got trouble? Ask for Rod." And I put my home number. A frightened young girl called the next day.

It should have lasted forever. The girls came to me like sheep, never telling a soul. Sheila was the only one I left where she lay. The others I wrapped in a rug and dumped in the woods for critters to eat. As the years went by, I rode a bus from campus to campus, taking a room in a motel, before posting my invitation. Business was brisk. The money was good.

But then, it all came to an end in late 1973. Once these girls could go to a doctor, my opportunities dwindled. I wasn't the type of guy they'd go with willingly. Not like Buddy.

My mother went to D.C. to protest with her church cronies. I loved her enthusiasm—fighting for my little projects that way. Ha! I stayed home with the old man and had a few drinks—laughing when we saw her on TV marching in front of the Supreme Court her face contorted with righteous indignation for all those unwanted fetuses.

"At least she's bitching at someone besides me," my dad said as he tossed back a shot.

I raised my glass and chuckled, "Go Mom!" The woman really hated sin but she didn't know a thing about it. All she knew was virtue. You never caught her sparing the rod. Oh no! I looked at the scars on my hand where she virtuously doused it in boiling water when I was four and pissed the bed. I swallowed the booze in one gulp.

Dad drifted off, snoring loudly. I switched off the TV. In my bedroom, I took my scrapbook out of the closet. It was wrapped up inside my baby blanket. I put it around my neck and rubbed the soft blue fleece against my cheek, the scrapbook in my lap. I didn't buy a Polaroid until I'd been at it for a year, so the first fifteen pages were just panties—mounted, neatly labeled with name and date. I touched Sheila's panties and remembered—even after all of these years. I lifted the album to my face. Her scent was gone now. I paged through the book, fingering the underwear, enjoying the pictures. I loved my girls.

I didn't know what to do next. I was thirty-one years old and my years of easy sin were over. I'd never had a job. I'd never lived by myself. I couldn't go back to the blankness I felt before *Shangri-la*. I sat on my bed, my back against the wall, my knees against my chest—sucking on my mother's Pall Mall.

I heard her come in around 2am. "What are you doing in here? Get your butt to bed," she said to my father. He belched. I cracked my door and peered at them as she hustled him into their room, muttering about the evils of drink. Even after a ten-hour bus drive, she was full of virtue. She put him to bed and within a few minutes, he was snoring again. Around 3, I heard the springs of their bed squeak as she climbed in beside the old man.

I tiptoed down the hall, my loafers in one hand, the scrapbook in the other. I stuffed newspapers under their door and wet it down with gasoline I'd siphoned from the old man's car. I lit a match and backed away as flames devoured the door. I was half way down the block when I heard her shriek. I was sitting on a bench at the train station, when I heard the fire engines wail. I hugged my scrapbook to my chest. Oh, but the wages of sin were sweet.

NOTE: Wages of Sin is the prologue to a psychological thriller, *Username*.

# SAPPHIRE LAKE

Ruby stood alone on the east bank of Sapphire Lake squinting into the sunset. Oblivious to the fiery sky, anger twisted inside her. She hated him. HATED him. The shades were drawn in the cottage across the water. Both the front and back doors were locked. She had tried each of them twice already—once right after he drove off down the dusty road in his gleaming new SUV, and then again after lunch when he hadn't answered his cell phone. She'd left four increasingly erotic messages one right after the other on his phone mail.

No response.

In frustration, she dialed the empty house. The endless ringing fueled her agitation and aroused her passion. She imagined him reading porn magazines by the stone fireplace in the house, hiding from her—ignoring her. Maybe he was lying on his bed thinking about some perverted slut, stroking himself. Maybe he was sitting at his computer whiling away the hours talking to other women. Maybe he went to work like he said.

"YOU BASTARD!" She screamed into the crisp silence. "You lying son of a bitch!" Her voice startled the ducks and geese floating on the smooth surface of Sapphire Lake and they rose en masse, their wings beating the cool evening air. "I HATE YOU, PETE TOWSON. I'll show you who you are dealing with. I'll SHOW you."

She dropped to her knees sobbing. She ripped small tufts of grass out of the ground and threw them into the air. Her shrieks faded into the soft lapping of the water. After a few minutes, she stood up and wiped her eyes with the hem of her thin cotton blouse. Gritting her teeth, she marched back towards her Aunt June's palatial log cabin.

The chrome kitchen welcomed her with a fluorescent glow. She found the quart of Chocolate Chip Cookie Dough Häagen-Dazs in the walk-in freezer. The long-handled stainless steel spoon hung from a rack over the stove. She went out onto the screened-in porch and lay back on a lounge. She could just make out Pete Towson's cottage in the late afternoon shadows across the lake.

"I'll give you one more chance!" She dialed the cell phone again.

"This customer is out of range." An electronic voice informed her.

"I warned you, asshole." She peeled the lid off the ice cream and fought to make a dent with the spoon. Eventually, the whole quart came loose from the package—impaled on the scoop. She held it in front of her with both hands and licked it like a lollipop. "Show you!" She murmured as she sucked and bit at the frozen dollop. Her lips stung with the cold and her teeth ached.

The ice cream began to melt and stream down the long handle of the spoon onto her arms, staining her blouse. She closed her eyes and concentrated on the smell of the chocolate, the sugary taste—the doughy texture in her mouth. She grunted with pleasure and lapped noisily.

His headlights flashed in her eyes as he turned into his driveway across the lake. She had been so engaged in the comfort of food that she hadn't heard his truck approaching. The soft thud of the Jeep door slamming carried across the water.

She let the remnants of the Häagen-Dazs drop onto the tile of her Aunt June's porch and, with sticky fingers, tapped his number on the keypad of the phone. It rang twelve times. No answer.

"Where is he? Where IS he?" She dialed again.

"Ruby, what are you doing?" He stood at the screen door, panting lightly.

"Where have you been?" She cried.

"Working. I told you I would be working today."

"But you've been gone so long! I couldn't find you. I couldn't call you." She stood frozen a few feet from the screen door.

"Let me in, Ruby."

"No!" She backed away.

"Then what do you want me to do? I have a job. I have a life." He scratched at the screen with his fingernails. She jumped.

"You are my life." She shrugged.

"No. No, I'm not. I'm just your lover."

"How can I trust you?"

"I don't know—but you are going to have to—or let me go. It's been a long day. I'm going home. You let me know which it's going to be." He backed away from the door and turned towards the path that encircled the lake.

"NOOOOOO!" She ran to the door and fumbled with the lock. She caught up with him near the edge of the water. She threw her arms around his neck and pressed her trembling body against his.

"Ruby, baby." He sighed and stroked her hair as she cried. "We can't keep doing this, honey." He kissed her eyes, then her mouth. "What is THIS?" He licked the Häagen-Dazs from her lips—sucking her tongue for a long hungry time. She fumbled with his trousers while he licked her cheeks. He pushed her down in the grass there on the edge of Sapphire Lake. He grabbed one thin hand and sucked the stickiness off her fingers—his tongue snaking between each digit. She wrapped her legs around his waist and drew him into her body while he continued to enjoy her chocolate sweetness.

Afterwards, she rebuttoned her stained blouse and pulled her long skirt down to cover her thighs. She lay in his arms—her anxieties temporarily assuaged. Their love was perfect. More perfect than with that bastard Norman Meeks. Even more perfect than Roger Beasley. Or Mark Reasoner who'd left her for that cow Lottie Sears. They always said it wasn't another woman when they left her, but she knew better. Men played games. All of them. She rolled onto her side to stare at Pete's profile. She knew he would leave her eventually.

He turned to smile at her. "Do you feel better now?" He stretched in post-coital bliss.

"I know I'm a poop. I can't help it. I hate being alone. I start out okay. Then I start thinking about what you might be doing. And I need to hear your voice. I need to know that you aren't—doing it with anyone else. I couldn't bear that, Pete. The idea of you touching someone else like you do me tears me apart. If I could just hear your voice, then I'd know what you were doing." The moonlight illuminated the desperation in her eyes. "If you'd just answer your cell phone, then I'd be okay."

"They won't let us keep our cell phones on when we are at some of the construction sites. I have phone mail, just leave me messages."

"But I need to know what you are doing!" She cried.

"Don't push me, Ruby."

"If you aren't doing anything you shouldn't, then why won't you answer me?"

"I work when I'm working, Ruby." He stood and stretched. His body embarrassed and amazed her. She reached up to cup his buttock—muscular, silken. She couldn't get over the way men paraded around in front of her naked. She liked the intimacy of it—but then she got to thinking about the other women who must have experienced the same intimacies and it made her mad. Nothing was special with men. Nothing.

Pete took two steps forward and plunged into the water. He swam out towards the middle of the lake.

"I can't believe you are doing that!" Ruby called to him.

"It's great after you get used to it. Come on in."

"I'm not going in there without a swimsuit."

"Ruby, you don't own a swimsuit. Come on, it'll be fun."

"I'm not doing it. You come out."

"Forget it." He turned and swam towards his cottage on the opposite shore.

Ruby jumped to her feet. "You left your clothes here." She gathered them up and ran alongside the water.

"I don't care."

"Where are you going?"

"Home."

"Don't you want to eat? Maybe we could go down to Denny's in town?"

"Ruby, I'm tired. I want to go to bed."

"But it's early yet. We could watch TV together."

"Not tonight." His feet found the bottom of the lake and he stood up. The water was waist high. Ruby rounded the corner and met him on the small sand beach in front of his house.

"But you must want to be with me. We just made love."

"There's more than just Sapphire Lake between us, Ruby." He splashed into shore and walked up to her.

"No, we love each other." She said.

He took his clothes from her. "Ruby, you are like a vulture waiting for a sick animal to die. You are always at me."

"No, I'm not. I'm not at you."

"You follow me everywhere. You look in my windows. You call my phones constantly."

"I just want to be with you. That's all."

"I know, baby. But you're just too much. I can't stand it."

"I knew from the first time that I saw you, Pete. I knew we'd get along."

"But that's just it, Ruby. We don't get along. We have nothing in common. We don't do anything together but sex. Hell, you won't even go swimming with me."

"I'll change. I promise, I'll change."

"You said that the last time—and the time before that."

"But I love you, Pete."

"No you don't." He went inside. She rushed forward but he slammed the door in her face. The lock clicked.

"YOU BASTARD!" She screamed.

Nothing.

"I just want something that is mine. Is that so bad?"

He hadn't even turned on the lights. He was sitting in there in the dark. She turned to walk away. At least there was a chance now. At least they'd finally made love without a condom. Maybe that love would take root. Maybe there would be someone who belonged to her totally. Maybe.

"I HATE YOU, PETE TOWSON!" She shouted into the darkness. Something shiny lay in the sand in front of her. She reached down. It was a gold-plated pen-knife. It must have fallen out of his pants pocket as he carried his clothes into the house. She knew it was his. She could feel the engraving on the handle. She struggled to open it with her bitten down nails.

"I'll show you." She murmured as she dug into the shiny green paint of his SUV with the tip of the knife. "I'll SHOW you."

# UNFORGIVABLE

At first it was just a vibration—like a distant heartbeat, then the faint smell of smoke. Hedy opened her eyes. Someone stood at the foot of her bed.

"Mama?"

"I didn't mean to scare you." Alicia Jennings' cigarette glowed in the darkness.

"Why are you here? Is something wrong?" Hedy could just make out her mother's features in the gloom.

"You know why I came back."

"Tell him to leave me alone." Hedy pulled the quilt up under her chin.

"Comes a time when you have to let go of the past, Hedy. Forgive and forget—that's what I say."

"I don't know how to do that." Hedy avoided Alicia's eyes. "I don't think I can."

"He's your father. You owe him."

"I do?"

"Don't take that tone with me, young lady."

Hedy sat up in bed. "How can you defend him after what he did to you? To us?"

"That was years ago—he's paid for that."

"Maybe that's not up to you to say, Mama. You don't have to live with it every day."

Alicia stubbed out her cigarette in a china dish on Hedy's dresser. "He's changed."

"I hope so, for his sake."

"You are hard hearted, Hedy—just like he used to be." Alicia lit another cigarette and exhaled.

"Don't do this to me, Mama." Hedy flinched. Smoke wasn't her favorite thing. "Mama?"

Alicia was gone.

"For God's sake, will this nightmare never end?" Every time her father's case came up for review, Alicia came to plead for him.

Something sparkled in the mirror. Hedy threw on her robe and got up. It was the reflection of her mother's lighter setting in the dresser. It was still warm.

Holding it against her cheek, she examined her own reflection. The shiny scar started below her right eye, snaked down her jaw, crossed her upper chest and sliced her forearm from elbow to wrist. Time and several surgeries had minimized the grotesquerie, but it was an ugly reminder of the things she learned at her father's knee.

Sleep was no longer an option even though it was only six-thirty in the morning. She sighed and dropped the lighter into her robe pocket. In the living room, she curled up in front of the television under a blanket. Clay Jennings's face flashed on the screen. The documentary on his case was on Court TV again. She clicked it off before they showed the famous photograph of Ronnie Kowalski carrying her out of the flames. Thirty-eight years since that night and it was still in her face.

*She was kissing Ronnie Kowalski on the front porch swing when her father yelled from the back of the house, "YOU STUPID BITCH!"*

*Ronnie startled. "What the hell?"*

*She flushed. Couldn't she have one nice evening without them embarrassing her?*

*"STAY BACK!" A loud crash drowned out Alicia's voice.*

*"Should we do something?" Ronnie peered into the living room window. "Maybe they need help?"*

*"They're fine—just drunk."*

---

The doorbell woke her.

"Miz Jennings?" The white-suited man towered over her.

"What do you want?"

"I'm Gabriel Angelino?" His embossed business card included 'Esquire' after his name. "I represent Clay Jennings in his appeal?"

"There's nothing I can do, Mr. Angelino." She tried to close the door, but he blocked it with his briefcase.

"I need to talk with you, ma'am."

Irritated, she sighed and let him in. Usually she wore thick make-up, but she was in her nightclothes and her cheeks were clean. His eyes lingered on her scar. She resisted covering her face with her hand. Like he didn't know what happened. "Would you like a cup of tea?"

"Yes, ma'am. If you don't mind." He followed her into the kitchen and sat down at the table.

"Tell them that they can do anything they want. I don't care," she said as she put on the kettle.

"I'm afraid that's not good enough." He set his briefcase on the table. "He's not getting out until you forgive him. That's policy."

"I don't hate my father, Mr. Angelino. I'm not even mad at him. I moved on years ago. Okay?"

The lawyer took a file out of his briefcase. "It doesn't work that way. He's done his mandatory stretch, but now he has to get pardons from all the parties. Your mother indicated her willingness to forgive him years ago. You are the only one standing in his way."

*Alicia's scream raised goose bumps on Hedy's neck.*

*"We need to help her," Ronnie stood up.*

*Hedy gripped his arm. "I'll go see what's going on."*

*"But what if she's hurt?"*

*"Go home, Ronnie." She gave him a push. "She won't want you in there."*

*He backed away. "What if you need me?" He called from the sidewalk.*

*"I won't." She turned and went inside.*

Hedy poured hot water onto the tea bags inside each mug. "The state took care of all that right after it happened. It wasn't up to me then, I don't see why I have anything to say now."

Angelino held up a death warrant. "Your father paid his debt to the state twenty-nine years ago when he was executed."

"Closure." Hedy served his tea and sat down across from him. "That's what they said anyway—but of course, whether he's alive or whether he's dead doesn't change anything for me."

"It was only the beginning for Mr. Jennings." Angelino handed her the record of her father's progress through the celestial courts. "As you can see, the clerk assigned him to me that same night. I presented his case a few days later and he moved to his current accommodations immediately after adjudication."

She rubbed her eyes. "So, is it like a prison for ghosts?"

"You are dealing with a whole other organization now, Miz Jennings. Different rules, different punishments, different opportunities."

*The struggle in the kitchen escalated. Another crash. Scuffling. Screams, grunts and a strange gurgling sound. Heart pounding, Hedy burst through the door. Her mother writhed on the table trying to ward off the long butcher knife clutched in her father's hand.*

*"NO!" Hedy froze in the doorway. "Stop it, Daddy!"*

*The knife sliced through Alicia's fingers and hit the table beside her head. Something wet splattered Hedy's cheeks. Stunned, she wiped her face with the back of her hand. Blood!*

*Without thinking, Hedy tackled him screaming. "You're killing her, Daddy!"*

*"It's her own damned fault." Clay swung the knife in a wide arc, slashing Hedy's cheek. "She made me do it."*

*"Hedy," Alicia moaned, pink bubbles frothing from her nostrils. "Go get help."*

*"YOU STUPID BITCH." Clay Jennings lifted the knife over his head, aiming at Alicia's heart.*

*Hedy tried to push him away. "Don't you hurt my Mama!"*

*Clay flung her against the wall and she fell hard against an overturned chair. Her feet slipping on the bloody linoleum, she struggled to get up.*

*Alicia's scream was more of a wheeze. "Hedy, stay back!"*

*Clay Jennings plunged the knife into Alicia's chest just as Hedy jumped between them.*

"What happens next?"

"He'll be reassigned to a new body if everyone agrees that he's ready."

"Ready?" Hedy frowned.

"He's been through a lot."

"Has he?"

Angelino tapped the paper. "He's learned to accept responsibility for his choices. He understands that there are consequences even when a course of action is justified."

"Oh yes, it was our fault. We got in his way. We made him angry."

Gabriel Angelino raised an eyebrow.

She folded her arms across her chest. "You think I'm bitter, don't you?"

He shrugged.

"I'm not."

"Then why can't you forgive him?"

"I don't know how, Mr. Angelino. I don't even know what forgiveness is." She leaned her head on her hands.

"What do you think it is?" His voice was kind.

"At first, I thought it was letting go of the emotion. Moving on with my life. Not being angry—but then that is about me. What good does that do him? He doesn't get a pass just because I'm doing okay."

Angelino's nod was noncommittal.

"Then I thought that it was about putting things right—but there is no do-over here. My mother has been dead my whole adult life. I spent my twenties in hospitals—first to fix my body, then to fix my mind. Then there were the trials, the appeals—waiting for his execution. Getting over his execution." She sniffed. "He can't give me back my youth, Mr. Angelino—or my mother."

"No, he can't." Angelino sighed.

"Someone once told me there was peace to be found in amnesia. I tried everything from meditation to hypnosis—but how do I forget my mother's face that night? How do I forget that blade slicing into me? Or the smell of the blood? Do you know what it's like when someone you love wants you dead, Mr. Angelino?"

The tall man's eyes were damp.

She blew her nose on a paper napkin. "Actually, I don't want to forget. Those memories make me cautious—wise."

"Wisdom comes at a price," Angelino agreed.

"And even if I DO forget, how does that help my father?"

"Has nothing to do with him, that's for sure."

*The pain didn't start right away. She lay on the kitchen floor—numb, bleeding. She thought she heard Alicia's last breath. Clay staggered around the room, sobbing. "Look what you made me do, you bitch." He slapped Alicia's cheeks, trying to revive her. "Don't you dare die on me."*

*Hedy gritted her teeth, hoping he would pass out before she did.*

*Dropping the knife, he dragged Alicia's body off the table and fell to the floor with it, cradling her in his arms. "Don't leave me, baby."*

*In the distance, a siren distracted him. Through half closed eyes, Hedy watched him. Drunk, distraught and frightened, he arranged Alicia on the floor beside him—straightening her legs, smoothing back* her hair. On all fours, he crouched over her—wailing. "ALICIA!"

The siren grew louder. Clay Jennings quieted, listening. Wiping his nose on the back of his hand, he lumbered to his feet and looked around. The evening newspaper was on the table, Alicia's last cigarette smoldering in the ash tray beside it. He wadded up the top sheet—then the second one.

Using the cigarette butt, he lit sheet after sheet and tossed them around the room until the thin curtains over the sink ignited. Still sobbing, he lay down beside Alicia.

Smoke filled the room quickly. Hedy closed her eyes, knowing that she was going to die soon. She felt the heat on her face and heard the flames crackling. Her father coughed. She opened her eyes. He got to his feet and stumbled out the back door, gasping for breath.

"Bastard," she thought.

Angelino laid a thin white envelope on the table in front of her.

Hedy wiped her eyes. "What happens if he gets a new body? Will I have to spend the rest of my life looking over my shoulder?"

"He wouldn't do that."

She bit her lip. "What's to stop him?"

"Well, he'll be a baby for one thing. Not much chance he'll come track you down for many years to come."

"Is that supposed to comfort me?"

"He won't remember the incident after he moves on to his new family. Only the psychic growth from his years in purgatory will remain."

"So he gets to forget?"

"He's been punished—twice."

"When do I get paroled, Mr. Angelino? When do I get to sleep through the night without thinking about what he did to my mother? When do my scars go away?"

"I have no answers for you, Miz Jennings." He pointed to the envelope in front of her. "You'll do what you do. It's no skin off my nose either way."

She ran her finger across the surface of the letter. "What do I have to do? Sign a paper?"

Angelino grunted. "I hardly think that your signature means much one way or another. It's what's in your heart that matters."

"Should I open it?"

He shrugged.

Trembling, she picked up the letter. She never spoke to her father after that horrible night. He never tried to contact her either—not while he was on death row and, unlike Alicia, no ghostly visits since. She wasn't sure she wanted to know what he had to say for himself. She wasn't sure she could bear it.

A single piece of paper was inside the envelope.

"HEDY." Clay Jennings never wrote in cursive—only thick, primitive printing. She didn't doubt the note was from him.

"I FACE AN ETERNITY OF SUFFERING. ONLY YOU CAN GIVE ME ANOTHER CHANCE. HAVE MERCY ON ME, DAUGHTER."

She looked up at Gabriel Angelino. "It's not much, is it?"

"It took him a lifetime to write that."

"Yes, he's very proud."

"Sometimes you have to consider what a person has to give." Angelino's voice was soft. "A half-empty container is empty long before a full one."

A sob caught in her throat like a hiccup. "And you expect more of me, Mr. Angelino?"

"I think you expect more of yourself."

"Ronnie Kowalski broke into that burning house to save me. He beat the flames out of my clothes with his bare hands. He was with me every day during my recovery. His scars are as deep as mine—and try as I might, I can't squeeze out one ounce of affection for him." She held up the letter. "But this crazy son of a bitch who thinks he can reach into my heart and crush it whenever he wants, I adore. It doesn't seem fair."

"Sometimes there are no good choices, Hedy—only a bunch of bad ones."

She stiffened. It was the first time Angelino had used her given name. "And no matter what I choose, there will be a penalty."

"Yes—and a reward."

She dug Alicia's lighter out of the pocket of her robe. "Some rewards aren't worth the pain, Mr. Angelino." She held her father's letter over the flame.

"What shall I tell him?" The tall man closed his briefcase and stood up.

"Tell him that I understand—and that I'm sorry."

Watch for Joyce Faulkner's psychological thriller: *Username*

## Other Books by Joyce Faulkner

*In the Shadow of Suribachi*, 2006 Military Writers Society of America Gold Medal for Historical Fiction
*Losing Patience*, 2006 Honorable Mention, Writers' Notes Magazine
*For Shrieking Out Loud*

## Coauthored with Pat McGrath Avery

*Role Call: Women's Voices*
*Sunchon Tunnel Massacre Survivors*, 2010 Gold Medal Branson Stars and Flags Book Award
Contact Joyce Faulkner at
JoyceKFaulkner@gmail.com

## Books by Pat McGrath Avery
*The Sharon Rogers Band: Laughed Together, Cried Together, Crashed & Almost Died Together*
*They Came Home: Korean War POWs Tell Their Stories*
*Letters from Korea: A Story of the Korean War*
*Tommy's War*
Contact Pat at patmcgrathavery@gmail.com
Website: www.patmcgrathavery.com
Blog: www.iwritemyworld.com
Facebook: patmcgrathavery